This book belongs to

_____

YOU ARE
Two

Sara O'Leary

artwork by
Karen Klassen

Owlkids Books

So much has changed
in just a year.

You are two!

First you could walk
and now you can run.

In the blink of an eye,
    you are up and down the stairs.

From the day you were born,
  we chose your clothes for you.

But now you have your own ideas
about what looks best.

Now that you are two,
    you sit right up at the table.

You can use your own spoon.
To eat with and to call for more.

You have words now.

And they tell us what matters to you.
Toy. Book. Apple.

Hug.

You call yourself by your own name.

You say "me." You say "MINE!"
(Sometimes you even share the things that are yours.)

Now that you are two, you are learning
about yesterday, today, and tomorrow.
You are forming memories
and making plans.

Wherever you go,
  your baby goes, too.

Even to dreamland.

When we sing songs,
you sing along.

And you make us happy when skies are gray.

You know so many things now that you are two.
What you know best is your own mind.

You are two,
and everything is changing so quickly.
But what will never, ever change
is our love for you.

Owlkids Books acknowledges the financial support of the Canada Council for the Arts, the Ontario Arts Council, the Government of Canada through the Canada Book Fund (CBF) and the Government of Ontario through the Ontario Media Development Corporation's Book Initiative for our publishing activities.

Published in Canada by
Owlkids Books Inc.
10 Lower Spadina Avenue
Toronto, ON M5V 2Z2

Published in the United States by
Owlkids Books Inc.
1700 Fourth Street
Berkeley, CA 94710

Library and Archives Canada Cataloguing in Publication

O'Leary, Sara, author
      You are two / written by Sara O'Leary ; illustrated by Karen Klassen.

(You are ; 2)
ISBN 978-1-77147-073-5 (bound)

      I. Klassen, Karen, 1977-, illustrator II. Title.

PS8579.L293Y687 2016   jC813'.54   C2015-908015-0

Library of Congress Control Number: 2016930938

The text is set in Clarendon LT Std.
Edited by: Jennifer Stokes
Designed by: Alisa Baldwin

 Canada Council
for the Arts

Conseil des Arts
du Canada

Canada

Manufactured in Shenzhen, Guangdong, China, in April 2016, by WKT Co. Ltd.
Job #15CB2344

A   B   C   D   E   F

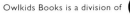 Publisher of Chirp, chickaDEE and OWL
www.owlkidsbooks.com

Owlkids Books is a division of Bayard
CANADA